this book
belongs to: _____

_____

_____

For my mom, Elaine —C.S.

For my mom, Jane —S.V.

For my Bee and her lovely little notes —H.R.

The illustrations for this book were made with pencil, paint, and Photoshop.

Cataloging-in-Publication Data has been applied for and may be obtained from the Library of Congress.

ISBN 978-1-4197-4960-5

Text © 2022 Courtney Sheinmel and Susan Verde
Illustrations © 2022 Heather Ross
Book design by Heather Kelly

Printed and bound in China
10 9 8 7 6 5 4 3 2 1

Abrams Books for Young Readers are available at special discounts when purchased in quantity for premiums
and promotions as well as fundraising or educational use. Special editions can also be created to specification.
For details, contact specialsales@abramsbooks.com or the address below.

Abrams® is a registered trademark of Harry N. Abrams, Inc.

ABRAMS The Art of Books
195 Broadway, New York, NY 10007
abramsbooks.com

Sallie Bee
Writes a Thank-You Note

words by **COURTNEY SHEINMEL**
and **SUSAN VERDE**

pictures by
HEATHER ROSS

ABRAMS BOOKS FOR YOUNG READERS

NEW YORK

On Monday,
there was a surprise
in the mail for Sallie.

It was not Sallie's birthday.

It was not a holiday.

It was just an ordinary day.

"Mom!" Sallie called.

"I need to send a text!"

After one minute, Sallie's mom was still on the phone.

And five minutes after that, she was still on the phone.

And ten minutes after *that*, she was *still* on the phone.

Sallie wrote down her text so she'd remember to send it.

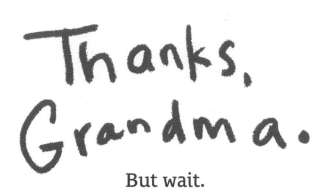

Thanks, Grandma.

But wait.

How would Grandma know what Sallie was thanking her for?

I love my new scarf. It has two of my most favorite colors.

And how would Grandma know how it made Sallie feel?

Outside, the wind was blowing.

It was the perfect time to have a new scarf.

"Mom, I need to send a looooooooong text!"

"That's not a text. That's a thank-you note.
Now all you need to do is sign your name."

"I also need to add some swirlies!" Sallie said.

Mom gave her an envelope and a stamp.

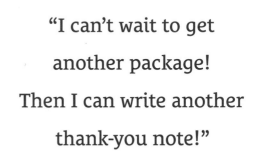

"I can't wait to get another package! Then I can write another thank-you note!"

The next day was Tuesday.
Sallie did not get any packages,
so she didn't have a reason to
write another thank-you note.

But . . .

She did get safely across the busy street.

Maybe *that* deserved a thank-you!

On Wednesday,

there were no packages.

But Sallie
borrowed an
umbrella.

Dear Bus Buddy,
 Thank you for letting me use your umbrella. When I got home, I was still dry. I hope your hood didn't get too wet.

Love,
Sallie

Thursday was
Taco Day at school.

Dear Ms. Myers,
Thank you for the scrumptious food. I'm happy we got to make our own tacos, because I don't like beans.
Love,
Sallie

And on Friday,
her brother kept his tarantula
in its cage all day.

On Saturday, there was another surprise in the mail.

It was an envelope, with lots of swirlies, addressed to Sallie Bee. She couldn't wait to open it.

Sallie felt so cozy, like
she was wrapped up in
a warm scarf with her
most favorite colors.

Dear Reader,

We are thankful that you read our book!

Do you have reasons to be thankful, just like we do, and just like Sallie does? Do you want to write a thank-you note? Here are some tips:

1. Decide who you are writing to.

2. Tell that person exactly what you are thankful for and why.

3. Say how it makes you feel.

4. Sign your name and give the note some style—maybe even some swirlies.

5. Write the person's name and address on an envelope, put a stamp on it, and send it on its way!

Love, Courtney & Susan